D1515052

this
·little·barron's·
book belongs to

....

....

For Harry

AE

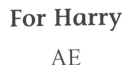

First edition for the United States and Canada published 1999 by
Barron's Educational Series, Inc.

Copyright text © Sally Grindley 1999
Copyright illustrations © Andy Ellis 1999

First published in Great Britain by Orchard Books in 1999.

All inquiries should be addressed to:
Barron's Educational Series, Inc.
250 Wireless Boulevard, Hauppauge, New York 11788
http://www.barronseduc.com

Library of Congress Catalog Card No.: 98-74976
International Standard Book No. 0-7641-0871-9

Printed in Italy

Time for Bed, Elephant Small

Sally Grindley • Andy Ellis

• little • barron's •

"Time for bed, Elephant Small,"
said Elephant Mom.

"But I want to play," said Elephant Small. And he chased around the room after Clockwork Mouse.

"Now wash your face and clean your teeth," said Elephant Mom.

But Elephant Small splashed Scaredy Cat with the sponge.

"I'll read you a story," said Elephant Mom.

"Goody," said Elephant Small as he jumped up and down on his bed and fell off with a bump.

BUMP!

"There was once an elephant called
Elephant Small," began Elephant Mom.
"And one day, he got lost."

"*Lost!*" cried Elephant Small. He jumped up and looked under his pillow. "I've lost my huggy thing!"

"*Here* it is," said Elephant Mom, and she pulled it out from under the bed. "Now snuggle down, and listen to the story."

She went on, "Sometimes Elephant Small
was naughty, but sometimes
he was very good."

"He's going to be good now,"
said Elephant Small.
"Hurray," said Elephant Mom,
and she finished her story.

"Can I see the moon before I go to sleep?"
yawned Elephant Small.

Elephant Mom opened the curtains.

"Goodnight, Moon," murmured
Elephant Small.
"Sleep tight, Elephant Small," said
Elephant Mom.

But Elephant Small
was already fast asleep.